THE LAST TRUE DAGGER DANCER OF NADUS

Callum Rushworth is an author, who lives in the United Kingdom with his wife, his pet rabbit, and tortoise. Since a young age, he has loved writing stories. Now as an adult he has the time and ability to make them come to life. Contained in this book is one such story.

Kiran

Happy Reading

C. *illegible* :)

Thank you for the Support

By Callum Rushworth

The Dark One Chronicles

The Summoner

Tales of Veridia

The Last True Dagger Dancer of Nadus

The Last True Dagger Dancer of Nadus

Callum Rushworth

For more information please contact
callumrushworth.writing@gmail.com

Paperback ISBN: 979-8-29931-653-7

FOR MY WIFE REBECCA.

I COULD DO NONE OF THIS WITHOUT YOU.

AND NESS, YOU KNOW WHO YOU ARE.

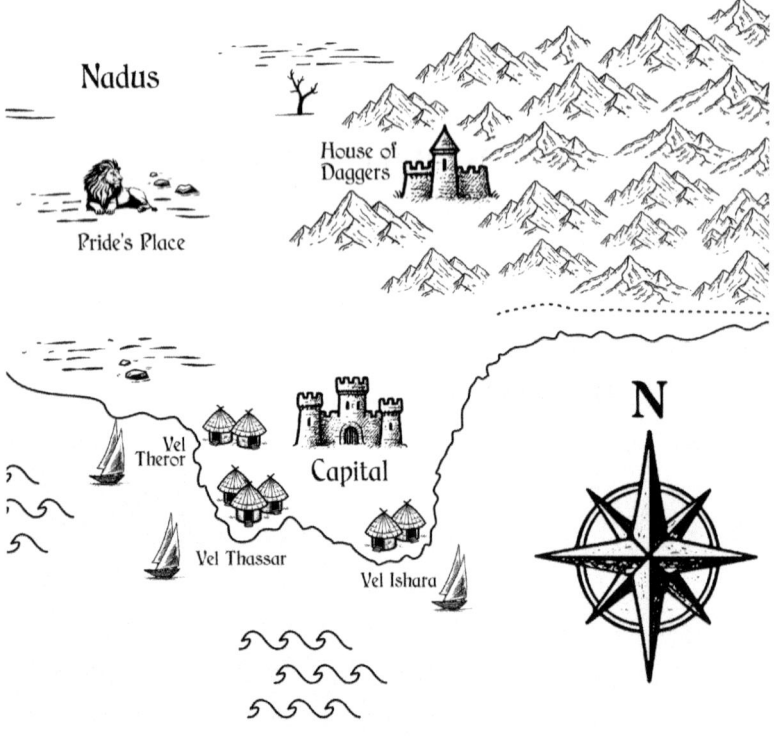

THE DAGGER DANCERS

The *Dagger Dancers* of Nadus were not soldiers, nor guards, nor spies. They were the Empress's justice, delivered at the end of a sharpened blade. To the common people they were known only as *Dancers*, but to those who called the dark Pyramid of the Capital home, they were called sisters.

They wore no crests, they carried no banners. It was only their twin daggers that marked them. Every *Dagger Dancer* trained from childhood within the obsidian walls of the Black Pyramid that overlooked the Capital, a desert jewel rising from the golden sands, that wrapped itself around their home.

The *Dancers* were an order like any other, exclusive yes, but not mythical. After all they were only human, just like the rest. But the people, they loved a myth.

Mothers whispered tales to restless children, of black-veiled protectors who lived in the shadows. Merchants left trinkets and spice at the feet of the Black Pyramid, offerings of protection and criminals told stories of sudden deaths and disappearances in alleyways. And though none had ever truly seen a *Dancer*, their stories spread throughout Nadus.

Each *Dagger Dancer,* upon completion of their Final Rites, was given one thing: an enchanted relic. No two were the same. One bore a ring that whispered lies into the ears of enemies. Another carried daggers that drank sound itself. One girl, pale-eyed and quiet, bore a chain that let her walk among shadows. Chiara had none of these things.

Her training had begun at eight years old. She remembered little before that, a sunburnt house, a mother with cracked hands, a brother that she might have imagined. The Black Pyramid became her home, her world, her cage. Every day was the same. Wake before dawn, spar until bleeding, meditate, memorise, serve tea to those who have passed their initiation. Run, learn the anatomy of the human body. Train again.

At twelve, she found Ness.

A golden jaguar cub, half-starved and snared by a hunter's trap outside the Pyramid walls. She had no idea how it had gotten so close to the Capital without being seen. No one had seen a golden jaguar in generations. The beast should have killed her. It didn't. Instead, it blinked at her, amber eyes glowing faintly in the dark, and let her free it. She killed the hunter, it was the first time she had taken a life. It wasn't the last. Something in the cub called out to her, reached for her, and when she reached back a miracle happened. They bonded. A soul-bond with an animal was another story that was told to children, that there were those who could speak to animals, and could hear them speak back. Chiara like everyone else hadn't believed in those stories, until the cub spoke to her. *Thank you,* that was all it had said, but it was enough.

Chiara hid her in the caves and tunnels of the desert behind the Pyramid, feeding her scraps and water. She named her Ness, after an old Nadusian word for flame. She taught her to stay silent, and Ness taught her how to stalk. She found herself sneaking out of the Pyramid more and more to spend time with her companion. The world seemed a lot less lonely from then on.

She told no one. Not even Selene. Especially not Selene.

Selene was everything Chiara wasn't. Confident, deadly, sharp-tongued. The daughter of a noble who had fallen from grace and been given to the Pyramid as penance. She was fierce, focused, flawless.

They trained together, fought together, even ate together. She was the sister she never had, a year older, but her best of friends within the order.

The order. Protectors of the people, the Empress's justice and the knives that guarded her back. But if the empress was truly immortal, as her nearly 1,000 year reign suggested, why would she even need protecting? That was the question that flitted through Chiara's mind when her faith was at its lowest, and the training didn't seem worth it.

Chiara moved like smoke through the alleyways of Vel Thassar, her hood low and steps silent. The town was half-asleep, caught in that transitional hour between wine and headache, where lovers stumbled home on aching feet and the night watchmen leaned too heavily on their spears. Salt clung to the stonework, carried on the southern breeze, and beneath her sandals, the bricks were still warm from the previous day's sun.

Ness padded along the outskirts of the town. Anyone who might have looked Chiara's way would have seen only a girl, hooded and hurried, clutching the folds of her dark wrap tight around her frame. No one would have known she was not alone. She never was.

This is reckless, Ness whispered in her mind. *Again.*

"He doesn't know," Chiara muttered aloud, voice low, the words stolen by the wind. "He thinks I'm just a servant. Anyways, I'm allowed out, it's not like they count us. As long as I'm back for morning drills, and can still stand up straight to take a beating, no one cares."

They will. Sooner or later.

Chiara didn't respond to that. Not because Ness was wrong, she never was, but because they both knew she'd come anyway. They could lock the Pyramid and post guards, do roll call throughout the night, and she would still find a way to come down to Vel Thassar. It had been seventeen days since she'd last seen Ramos. Seventeen days of sand, blood, drills, poison lessons, and endless

10

sparring matches beneath the devil eyes of the High Blades. Seventeen days of torture, seventeen days of missing him. In that time, she had snapped another initiate's wrist, slit the throat of a goat for no other reason than it was expected of her, memorised three new poisonous plants, and learned how to hold her breath for four and a half minutes underwater. Which made quite honestly no sense to her, when had she ever even been near water except when she snuck out to see Ramos. Like tonight.

The sea was much closer now, she could smell it on the breeze. Chiara darted across the final street, taking care to keep her profile small enough to pass for a servant girl or some incense runner. Her hands were trembling beneath the folds of her cloak.

He's close. Ness purred in her mind. *Do you want me to go hunt? For privacy, of course?*

If you're hungry just say you're hungry. But yes, go hunt.

Try to be back in time for the scraps. Don't forget, tonight is your last night as an initiate, you cannot be found missing when they come to induct you.

Ness was right, again. On every initiate's 21st celebration of their birth, they were given their final rites, a final challenge. Pass and become a *Dancer*, fail and you'd be too dead to care. Chiara rounded the corner to the little stone house at the bottom of the lane, the one with blue shutters and an old rusted lantern above the door. She tapped once, twice, paused and then once again. It was their secret knock, the one he'd taught her all those years ago.

The door opened before she could blink.

She smiled at Ramos, who stood there bleary eyed but smiling back. His shirt was unlaced and stained with old dyes. He always smelled of salt and polished wood. Her heart fluttered at seeing him, only three years her elder, but he had matured just as nicely as reserva chianti. He'd always been a good looking boy, its what shallowly had drawn her too him those years ago. But now… Fuck!

His hands found her waist before her mouth found his, and she melted against him, grateful and reckless all at once. She felt Ness purr again in her mind.

Boundaries Ness, boundaries.

Sorry, its this Gazelle I've found, it's delicious. Chiara knew Ness hadn't found anything yet.

Go hunt. Now!

"I was starting to think you were dead," Ramos murmured against her ear.

"Not quite yet," she whispered back, shoving him backwards through the door, straddling him as he landed on the bed. They didn't talk much after that.

TALES FROM THE OLD WORLD

He made spiced tea later, once their sweat had cooled and her heart rate had slowed back down to a normal level. Chiara sat cross-legged on the edge of his bed, looking out at the sea which was visible through the slatted window. It was dark, but rolling peacefully. There was something about looking out at the sea that always found a way to calm her. Ramos stirred a clove into the tea, barefoot and humming some sailors' tune she didn't recognise.

"Something's changed around here. There's more whispering around the docks, and more people disappearing by the day. That why I was worried when I hadn't seen you for a while, I was worried the *Dancers* had taken you."

Chiara had to stifle a laugh. "The *Dancers*! Take me? Now why in the Empress's name would they do that?"

"I don't know," Ramos admitted. "People are disappearing by the day, and surely not all of them are risks to her eminence. I was just worried, that's all."

"I'm perfectly safe. Come here." She motioned him over with a smile.

"I met a trader from Vel Ishara," he said, handing her a cup. "He said they've seen ships come back from the west.

Not just stories. Actual sails."

Chiara sipped the tea, appreciating the warm burning sensation it left as it went down her throat and chest. "What did they bring?"

"Mostly stories and rumours. But there was gold too, Old Empire markings. Crates and crates of old wine and rum. It was all untouched. They say theres some sort of mass graveyard. Raul, a captain I spoke to said there was a reef formation and it looked like an entire armada had sunk. He sent down some divers and this is what they brought up." Ramos paused, taking a sip of his own tea. "He said if he'd have had more time, or more men he'd have searched the lot!"

She said nothing. There was nothing to say, the old empire had always been his dream. In the 5 years she'd known him he'd always wanted to sail west. But the poor son of a fisherman couldn't really afford to put those dreams into action. His father's ship could barely sail the shallows, let alone the depths of the great western seas. She let him dream though, it was something that always made him happy.

He crouched in front of her, his fingers brushing hers. "If I had a ship... I'd go. I'd go tomorrow. Just vanish over the edge of the world. I wouldn't even say goodbye."

"You'd vanish and not say goodbye to me?" she asked, giving him a look of mock hurt.

"I'd take you with me. Obviously."

She laughed softly. "Where would we go?"

He shrugged. "West, somewhere where we could live where no one knows us. Where we could live in peace. I could fish, and you could lie by the beach, drinking wine. And in the evenings we could relax by an open fire and struggle to keep our kids from touching the flames."

She looked away. "That place doesn't exist." *Fuck.* Kids, she knew that topic would come up one day. She'd hoped that it wouldn't have come up before she was inducted. Before she'd have to travel to the House of Daggers. Before she'd have to say goodbye. This had always had an expiry date, she'd known it. Clearly he hadn't.

Ramos leaned in and kissed the side of her neck, just once. "Then we'll build it."

He means it. Ness breathed into her mind again. This time she did truly have a Gazelle under her paws.

Are you always watching, is nothing private?

That thing he did with his tongue... can stay between you. I did make a catch, but it was hard with your thoughts working over time over the last twenty minutes. I don't mean to listen. We're connected, I can't just ignore you, especially when your mind screams like that.

Ness... That's... inappropriate. But fair, I'd never really thought about that, but when I'm just sitting in the Pyramid I do often follow you in your hunts.

I know, I feel you with me, always. But he does, you

15

know? He means it.

I know. And that's what makes this worse.

The jaguar didn't respond, and Chiara knew why. She didn't know how.

Chiara leaned forwards, wrapping her arms around Ramos's neck. "Not tonight, tonight I don't want a world building. I just want you."

Chiara left before dawn, her cloak clung to her shoulders, soaked through with the sea mist that rolled up the streets this early, like some sleeping beast. She could feel the sting of the salt it carried, biting at the corner of her eyes, as she picked her way through Vel Thassar's crooked streets. Behind her, the fishing boats were already dots against the gray horizon.

The town was waking around her, in that begrudging way that coastal places do. Shutters creaking open above her head, smoke beginning to curl from chimneys, weathered faces peering down onto the streets though muck stained windows. There was the all too familiar smell of brine mixed with yesterday's fish guts, creating that particular perfume that marked every fishing town she'd ever known. Her boots found the familiar paths without thought, avoiding the loose cobblestones that would clatter and announce her presence and departure. Looking up, the harbour master's bell tower loomed against the lightening sky, its bronze weathered into a coppery green. She didn't look back. She didn't linger, she never lingered. She'd learned long ago that staying too long in doorways only made the leaving harder. This time, this final time, she knew if she'd have tried to say goodbye, she wouldn't have left.

You're scared he'll leave too. Ness stated. She always had a way of getting to the root of her inner turmoil.

I don't know what I think, what I feel. This thing, whatever it is, always had an end date. I can only wish him the best.

You could have gone with him.

How? Run away from the order? Be realistic, Ness, the order is everything.

To you right now, maybe. It doesn't have to be.

We're getting closer to the Pyramid, you'd best return to your den, don't want anyone spotting you.

By first sunlight she'd reached the border markers, where the sand deepened and the scrub vanished. The climb from the port town to the Capital was harsh and long. Caravans took at least a day. On a bad day it took her a morning at most. She ran barefoot, her sandals tied to her belt, her legs lean with muscle from years of training. Ness padded behind her, untiring. The desert did not slow them.

The Black Pyramid rose from the dust like a god's fist. It was a monolith of midnight black stone, obsidian and ancient, every side slanted in such a way that it caught the sun and didn't let it go. It had always unsettled her how the light seemed to be absorbed by the place. There were no banners flying, no doors, no guards. Those who entered the Pyramid knew how, those that didn't and tried anyway vanished.

For the next part, she knew she would need her sandals back on. Part of being a *Dancer* was knowing what you needed in each environment, and for climbs, barefoot was an absolutely fucking not. Chiara climbed the switchback path up the southern side, keeping her breath steady for the rise. Ness bounded off in the other direction, to stay far outside the city's perimeter, beyond the red dunes. The Pyramid's enchantments were ancient and thorough. Had Ness entered, she would've been seen, felt, by the hundred eyes that lined these walls, magical and otherwise.

At the top of the path, Ness spoke into her mind for what would be the final time until she next left the Pyramid. *Someone's waiting.*

Chiara slowed, drawing the daggers from her side instinctively. Their weight was familiar, their pommels worn smooth from her grip. She thanked her foresight after leaving Ramos's to take her blades from her satchel and place them in their rightful home.

Then she saw the figure.

Sister Mariona stood beneath the outer arch, arms folded, her face half in shadow. Her robes were black, embroidered at the hem with crimson thread. Her silver circlet gleamed against her forehead. She did not smile.

"You were seen," she said matter of factly.

Chiara didn't answer. What could she say? She had been caught, and there was no use trying to talk a sister out of a punishment, in her experience it only made the consequences worse. Yes, better to keep your mouth closed and wait and see what they dispense.

"Vel Thassar is forbidden to initiates after nightfall."

Still, Chiara said nothing. Shit! Well perhaps that was all they knew of her little expedition. If they knew of Ramos she'd have opened with that, likely before opening him up. *Dancers* were off limits, and although she was not technically one yet, she did know the mortal danger she placed him under every time she went to see him.

"You've been summoned," Mariona said, with the tone of someone stating a punishment. "High Matron Catalina awaits you in the Hall of Blades."

Chiara's stomach dropped. Perhaps they knew of Ramos after all, or something even worse? She found her feet moving before her mind stopped racing.

"Now?" she asked, voice hoarse.

"Yes, Congratulations, initiate. You are to undergo your final rites."

Mariona turned and vanished into the Pyramid's shadow. All she could do was follow, and pray.

AN INITIATION

The halls of the Black Pyramid swallowed Chiara in silence as she passed through them. Her sandals whispered over the obsidian tiles, which were polished mirror-smooth, broken only by faint hieroglyphs that cut like veins through the stone. The glyphs pulsed sometimes, softly, dimly, as if the Pyramid itself had a heartbeat. They were a relic of a forgotten time, the Pyramid was older than the Empress herself, some say older than the land. The place had its secrets, and she cared not to uncover them. She kept her eyes forward. Dozens of initiates had already failed this final stage of training. They had all disappeared quietly, looking back on it, lots had.

She passed beneath the towering archways, each lined with golden lions, their mouths open in silent roars, and walked further still into the Pyramid's depths. Finally she reached the entrance to a side passage, guarded by statues. They were twin dancers, both with curved daggers, their poses frozen mid-leap. The House of Daggers expected perfection, only the very best could enter the Empress's service. Chiara's fingers itched to stroke Ness's fur, to feel that familiar press of warmth against her thigh. But it would likely be moons before she could risk seeing her again. If she passed the rites, if she lived.

Further down, a new passage opened, this one was lit with an amber flame. She stepped through and into the waiting hall of the Inner Circle. Twelve *Dagger Dancers* stood in silence, half-shadowed beneath the great torches. Only three were unveiled, the others wore obsidian masks etched with fangs. One of the unmasked stepped forward to greet her. Selene.

Of course it was Selene. Initiates were always greeted by twelve *Dancers* before being given their final test, before being inducted into the order. Their last rights. The newest Acolyte was by tradition the one to greet the passing initiate, and Selene had been promoted not three moons ago. Chiara hadn't seen or heard anything from her since that day, nearly a full season ago. She'd changed.

Her voice echoed around the small waiting hall. "Chiara of nothing, daughter of no one. You are summoned."

"I heard the summons," Chiara said quietly. Selene loved to rub the fact she was an orphan in her face any chance she got. The order was originally meant for those outcasts, orphans and the unwanted of the world, but in recent years it had become an aristocracy's pet project. There were now more third daughters of minor lords in its ranks than those who it was intended for.

"You are ready?"

"I am."

"Prove it."

Chiara knelt, bowed, and placed both daggers across her palms, blade to wrist. Selene moved like a shadow, her own dagger unsheathed. She touched its point to Chiara's forehead. "You know what is asked of you?"

"I do." She wished for nothing more, than for this perfunctory display to be over with.

"You are given this final task before you may join the House of Daggers."

"I understand."

Selene lifted the blade and pointed to the steps behind her. "Go below. You'll be briefed."

Chiara rose and descended the spiral steps. She didn't look back.

Below in the inner hall, the air was much cooler, and sharper. It was a circular room, with no doors, save the opening she entered through, and no windows. Stepping inside, the walls closed behind her, sealing her in. All that was inside was a single silver lantern and a woman wrapped in crimson silk. Her eyes were heavily lined with some dark powder which seemed to suck the light right out of the room. It gave Chiara the same ominous feeling the obsidian blocks of the Pyramid did. Was that the intended purpose she wondered? The woman did not rise when Chiara entered.

"You're late," said the woman.

Chiara frowned. "I was summoned not ten moments

ago." A rare mistake from her, say nothing, there's no talking them round.

"The summons came at dusk," the woman snapped.

Chiara said nothing. She couldn't explain why she hadn't received the summons at dusk to the woman, but at least if they didn't already know, then they didn't know about Ramos, about Ness.

"You'll go west to the central regions near the Steppe. There's been unrest. Another peasant rebellion."

"Another?"

"Some ex-soldier named Enan has been feeding the poor. Stirring up the idea that they deserve... more."

Chiara narrowed her eyes. "And we're to kill him?"

"Yes. Him, and any man or woman who calls themselves a rebel."

Chiara folded her arms. "I thought this was a mission of precision. Not a slaughter."

"Rebels have been popping up more and more lately. Villages across the Steppe, even towns along the coast have begun questioning their taxes, refusing payments. How is Nadus to fund its army, to protect its people's interests if everyone who wishes they were treated better took it upon themselves to claim that better life?

"They don't understand that the Steppes are free from bandits because our patrols make it so, that our waters are free from pirates because our navy makes that so. They abhor paying their due as they can't see that without it they'd have no money to give." She paused to let the point sink in. Chiara couldn't help but feel that this lecture was far from over.

"Take this Enan for example, he believes his town pays too much in levies of grain. He has taken to storing away parts of the harvest and lying to our collectors about how much they've taken. He doesn't know that we know, and our collectors certainly aren't aware of the deception, the dumb eunuchs. If we removed the patrols from that area, then some less well to do peasants from the town over would likely raid them to take more, and then they'd be without any. But that would be messy, and the Empress hates mess. Taxes beget order, order beget prosperity."

She coughed, taking a moment to clear her throat.

"Our order is not what it once was. If we are to protect our Empress's interests we will need to start acting with a firmer hand," The woman stared deeply at her, deep enough that Chiara wondered if she was trying to read her mind. "Besides, if I wished you to wipe out the entire village then you would do it, no questions asked, no reasons required. You are to be a *Dancer,* not a philosopher. You are to act as the Empress wishes, without hesitation. Do you understand?"

Chiara's stomach twisted, but she nodded. "Yes."

"Selene has chosen Alexia as your partner. You leave at dawn on the day of the new moon, two days from now. Put whatever you have in order, for pass or fail, you will not be returning to the Pyramid anytime soon."

Chiara bowed once and turned. The walls of the chamber opened on her approach, magic parting the stone like water. The air outside stung her lungs. She had to see Ness, she couldn't wait.

Chiara waited until the moon was at its peak before slipping away from the sleeping compound. Her sandals made no sound on the cobblestone paths. Down below, the narrow streets of the Capital stretched into silence, black and gold beneath the watchful eye of the Pyramid.

She took the alley route through the silk district, past curtained doors and blue lanterns, past shuttered perfume sellers and snoring gamblers. At the edge of the city wall, she climbed the old aqueduct where bricks crumbled under her weight and leapt into the darkness beyond.

Ness was waiting.

The golden jaguar lifted her head from the sand as Chiara approached. Her eyes glowed faintly under the stars.

You came late, Ness said, her voice a soft hum inside Chiara's mind.

"I was summoned."

The final trial?

Chiara nodded.

Ness padded close, her fur shimmering like moonlit fire. She pressed her heavy skull into Chiara's side.

"They want me to kill peasants. A man named Enan. He feeds the poor. And my orders are to cut him down."

Will you?

Chiara couldn't answer, she didn't know. Instead, she wrapped her arms around Ness and buried her face in the warm fur. "I had to see you before I left."

And Ramos?

Chiara swallowed. "I'll see him too."

Vel Thassar smelled strongly of salt and spiced wine in the early evening, as the day's work was ending and the night's drinking just beginning. Ships creaked in the harbour and gulls screamed over the rooftops. Chiara moved quickly and quietly between the carts and beggars, keeping her veil drawn low.

She found Ramos where he always was at this hour, at the edge of the fish market, loading crates for his cousin's shop. His sun-darkened arms strained beneath the weight of salted cod, and his shirt stuck to his back with sweat. She waited until the other workers had passed before stepping into the alley. He tensed at the sound of her footsteps and stood up straight, though not turning round. Strange, he didn't seem the type to scare easily. She cleared her throat. He turned and smiled instantly, a relieved smile, the type you'd give to someone who just saved your life.

"By the Empress! I hoped it'd be you," he said.

"Who else could it have been?" She asked, returning his smile.

"No one, anyone. It's getting strange out here. People are beginning to get scared to leave their houses. Of course that doesn't stop the drinkers."

"I have to leave soon, I'm sorry. I'm not sure if or when I'll be back. I couldn't leave without saying goodbye."

"I did wonder what had happened when you disappeared the other night."

"I've always found goodbyes easier if you don't have to say them."

"But this goodbye is different?"

"Yes." Chiara said, holding back the tears.

"You shouldn't have come." He said reaching out and wiping away one solitary tear that had fallen down her cheek.

"I had to."

He stepped forward and kissed her, quick and hard. They stood in silence for a while after, their heads pressed together.

"I wish you'd tell me," he whispered. "What it is, you do."

"You wouldn't understand."

"Try me."

Chiara pulled back. "I can't." There was much she wanted to add to that statement, like, *not because I don't want to, but for your own safety.* That her presence here

27

alone puts him in peril, but she could say none of that, and it would have to remain forevermore a prisoner in her thoughts.

Ramos sighed, then offered a half smile. "Someday I'm going to have my own ship. We'll sail wester than west and find the Old Empire. You'll see."

She reached up and cupped his face in her hands. "Promise me you'll wait?"

"I'd wait a thousand years for you."

They both knew it was a lie. The moment he had a ship, if she wasn't there, he'd sail away and not look back. She didn't blame him. She leant in and kissed him again anyways.

A DANCER AND A FARMER

Dawn bled gold across the Steppe that morning. There was something in how the southern winds whispered that gave Chiara pause. Was this truly the right thing to do? To kill a peasant whose only known crime was holding back grain from tax collectors? It seemed harsh for such a petty thing.

Alexia was already saddled and waiting at the edge of the Black Pyramid's outer gate. Her mare was a striking seal brown, nearly black save for its tanned points over its muzzle. It was restless. Alexia looked restless too, but with none of the worry over whether their cause was just or not. Chiara supposed that was the bit you lost when you became inducted. That sense of right or wrong, there was no room for such beliefs when you were ordered to distribute the Empress's justice.

"You're late," Alexia said.

"No one ever says that when she's early." Selene joked, striding out from behind the gate to mount her own youthful steel grey horse.

"I suppose the old one's mine?" Chiara asked as she walked over to the mature dappled snow-dotted white mare.

"Would you rather walk?" Alexia asked without a hint

29

of humour.

"She'll do just fine." Chiara responded, throwing herself over to straddle the horse.

She'd do just fine for supper, Ness added for Chiara's benefit. She had to stop herself from chuckling.

"Something funny?" Alexia snapped.

"Nothing, shall we begin?"

The older *Dancer* offered no smile. Her eyes were a pale grey, and her skin was darker than Chiara's. Most strangely she bore her daggers openly on her belt, rather than concealed like most *Dancers*. She kicked her horse into a trot and set off down the sand dirt track.

They rode in silence for much of the morning. The Pyramid faded slowly behind them.

The last ribbon of river vanished behind them before noon. It had narrowed and meandered until it seemed almost ashamed to exist, then sank into the thirsty earth, leaving behind only reeds and a scattering of dragonflies. By the time the sun reached its zenith, they were in the dry grasslands, rolling sweeps of gold and greeny brown that seemed to breathe under the wind's slow hand. How the grass survived here was anyone's guess, all Chiara knew for certain was that it did, and that was enough for her.

They crested a low ridge in the midafternoon, and Chiara's gaze caught on the lions. A pride of at least eight, sprawled in the sun along the shattered bones of a stone archway. The structure had been tall once. She imagined banners snapping in the wind, columns gleaming white in the noon light, but now it leaned and sagged, its base swallowed by the creeping dead grass. The lions owned it now, their tawny hides blending in with the ancient sand-swept stone.

One of the males, a thick-maned brute with a scar over his muzzle, lifted his head as the riders passed. His amber eyes met Chiara's across the distance, at least she thought they did. It felt as though he was looking into her very being. Alexia ahead of her hadn't even turned her head in the lion's direction.

Selene noticed Chiara looking and gave a faint smirk. "You always were easily distracted."

Chiara didn't answer. She wasn't in the mood for teasing.

They pressed on until the sun fell low, staining the west in deep orange. The shadows of the horses stretched long and sharp over the grass. That was when Alexia raised a hand and turned her mare toward a shallow depression in the land where a creek had once run. The bed was dry, its banks rough with windblown dust.

"This will do," she said, sliding from the saddle without waiting for agreement.

Selene swung down lightly and began unstrapping her packs. Chiara dismounted more slowly, stretching her legs. Her mare gave a low huff, grateful for the stop.

The air cooled quickly once the sun slipped toward the

horizon. Out here, the nights could bite harder than the days burned.

Chiara busied herself gathering firewood. The grasslands didn't offer much, twisted roots, thorny branches, and deadfall from stunted trees. But she made do. Ness's voice brushed against her thoughts. *That one doesn't like you.*

Which one? Chiara thought back.

The one who smells of steel dust. The pale-eyed one.

Alexia. And I noticed.

She's waiting for you to stumble.

Then I won't.

Ness rumbled her approval.

By the time Chiara returned, Selene had a small circle cleared for the fire. The flames took quickly, throwing long shadows across the creek bed. Alexia sat with her back to the firelight, her daggers lying on a cloth in her lap. She glanced up as Chiara set down the wood.

"You move too loudly," she said.

"In the grasslands?" Chiara asked. "Should I try to sneak up on the lions?"

Alexia's pale eyes narrowed slightly, but she didn't answer. She picked up one of her daggers and tested its edge with her thumb, then returned it to her lap.

Selene stirred the pot she'd set over the flames. The smell of lentils and dried meat rose into the cooling air. "Alexia thinks everyone moves too loudly," she said, without looking up.

Alexia's gaze flicked to her, but again she said nothing.

Chiara sat on her bedroll, stretching out her legs. Her thighs ached from the day's ride, not enough to make her complain, but enough to make her shift occasionally to ease the stiffness. She studied Alexia's face across the firelight.

"You've been watching me since we left the Pyramid," Chiara said at last.

Alexia met her eyes without hesitation. "That's my job."

"To watch me?"

"To watch everyone," Alexia corrected. "Especially those who haven't proven themselves yet."

They ate in near silence. The fire crackled, and the wind sighed through the grasses around them. Selene kept the conversation to practical matters, routes, distances, weather, though Chiara could see in her eyes she wanted to say more. The facade of the *Dancer* sat on her like borrowed clothing, ill-fitting, but necessary.

When the meal was done, Chiara lay back on her bedroll, staring at the stars. Out here, far from the glow of Vel Thassar, the night sky was a flood of light. She found the familiar constellations, the *Dancer*, the Crown, the Three Blades, and traced their lines in her mind.

She felt Ness's quiet presence at the back of her mind,

the jaguar's voice soft as breath. *She doesn't trust you.*

I noticed.

Then stop meeting her eyes. Makes predators nervous.

Does that make me prey? I'm not prey.

Neither am I, Ness said, her tone edged with a purr. *But it's not us who decides that, when we're unaware we are in a hunt.*

Selene finally broke the silence. Her dark eyes measuring, weighing the air between them. "We all serve the same Empress. That's what matters. What she calls justice, we carry out."

Chiara kept her gaze on the stars. "I didn't join to become blind," she said at last. "If I'm ordered to deliver justice, I want to see who it's falling on, and why. Anything less is… cowardice."

The older *Dancer's* eyes flicked up. "Careful, girl. That sounds like doubt."

Somewhere far off, a lion roared, and the sound rolled across the land like thunder stalling the tension.

"They're closer than I'd like," Selene said.

"They'll smell the horses," Alexia agreed. "But they won't come close unless they're desperate."

Ness's voice brushed against Chiara's thoughts again. *I could keep them away.*

Not now, Chiara told her. *Not here.*

"Rest now, tomorrow will be harder. We should reach the village by nightfall," Alexia said, before laying down on her own roll.

Chiara closed her eyes, letting the warmth of the fire seep into her bones. The night smelled of dust, smoke, and the faint trace of lions on the wind.

Sleep little one, I will keep the beasts from your door.

The village appeared as they crested a low ridge, a huddle of sun-bleached stone and thatch. No walls, no guard towers, only a scattering of fences meant to keep goats from straying too far.

The road was little more than a brown scar cutting through the dried wheat fields. Heat shimmered off the earth, seeming to bend the air in trembling waves. Chiara rode between Alexia and Selene, her fingers brushing the edge of her headscarf, feeling the coarse weave catch on her skin. They had dressed as traders. Simple tunics, worn boots, small satchels and, of course, concealed blades.

From up here, the place seemed almost peaceful. Almost. A woman stooped over a washboard. Two kids chased each other with sticks. Chickens scurried between their feet, scattering in little explosions of feathers. But there was a stillness beneath it all, a few glances lingered too long on the ridge.

Selene slowed, before dismounting. "We should hide the horses here."

"He knows we're coming?" Chiara asked, still scanning.

Alexia's lips barely moved. "No. But villages like this hear whispers long before feet arrive." She shifted the strap of her satchel. Her eyes flicked between doorways. "We go in as merchants. We ask for water. Selene leads."

They followed the curve of the road down, dust clinging to their calves. The smell of bread baking met them before they reached the first house. A boy darted past, staring openly at them before vanishing into an alley.

"They'll tell someone we're here," Chiara murmured.

"Good," Alexia replied. "Let's see who comes looking."

They passed between the houses, boots crunching softly on the dry dirt. Chiara kept her eyes moving, scanning the rooftops, windows, and narrow passages. Regardless of her feelings on the mission, they'd been sent to deliver justice, and if Enan was a rebel and they went in unprepared they'd be dead. Her eyes caught on a man mending a fence. He paused, squinting at them, then went back to work.

The well stood in the centre of the village. Selene approached it with the slow, deliberate rhythm of someone who has walked too far under a hot sun. She lowered the bucket, filled a clay cup, drank, and then handed it to Chiara, flashing a smile to an elderly woman sitting watching them.

As Chiara sipped, her eyes drifted across the square. A low building sat apart from the others, with a narrow porch shaded by a faded awning. Two men leaned against the wall, one sharpening a small hatchet, the other idly carving at a piece of wood. Both watched them without speaking.

"That'll be his house," Alexia said, leaning in.

"How do you know?" Chiara asked.

"Look at their hands. Hardly the well set calluses of a farmer. They're soldiers. Guarding something I'd bet."

"We circle east. Find a back way in," Selene said without looking at them.

They left the well, weaving between the houses until the square was behind them. The narrow lanes twisted inward, shaded by strips of cloth strung between buildings. The air smelled heavily of hay, bread and something sharper. When they reached the edge of a goat pen Selene paused and nodded toward a side path. "That way."

It took them behind a low building. From there, they could see a small back door, half hidden by a curtain of hanging laundry. A woman knelt nearby, scrubbing a shirt. They were about to move when a figure exited through the door. The woman didn't even look up, like he wasn't really there. Chiara was questioning her vision herself as she caught a glimpse of the man before he pulled his hood up and skulked off down an adjoining alley. His skull was shrunken, and his eyes! His eyes were purple. She had never seen anything like it.

"Not our target," Alexia whispered. "Although should be cautious, it seems Enan has some friends in dark places. The Empress must be informed of this."

Selene moved first, passing silently until she reached

37

the shadow of the wall. Chiara followed, focusing on keeping her steps soft. Selene slipped inside first. Alexia motioned for Chiara to follow.

The interior was incredibly dim in contrast from the brightness she came in from. It smelled faintly of woodsmoke. A single table stood in the centre of the room, cluttered with a loaf of bread, a half cut wheel of cheese, and a scattering of herbs.

A man sat at the far wall, mending a leather strap under a candlelight. His back was to them and he didn't turn, but only lifted his head. "You've come to kill me?"

Selene stepped forward, silently sliding her blade down from her sleeve. "Well we're not here to talk."

Enan rose slowly, palms open. "I am not your enemy," he said. "I bled for Nadus when the Empress called. I fought on her borders when the sands ran red. And now I treat the sick and elderly. I feed starving children. Is that a crime?"

He wasn't what she'd pictured, not a scarred brute or a fire-eyed zealot, but a man in his middle years, hair streaked with grey, the lines on his face carved deep by sun and worry.

"Your hands are dirty with rebellion," Alexia said flatly. "Kill him, Chiara."

Chiara's throat tightened as she released her daggers from her sleeve, they fell smoothly into her hands. They felt wrong though, an extension of the training beaten into her, yes, but suddenly too heavy.

Enan must have seen it, the hesitation, because his eyes widened with a desperate sort of hope.

"You're young," he whispered, his voice breaking a touch. "Too young to be so cruel. Am I to be your initiation? Look at me, I am no rebel. I command no army, have no banners waving at my back. I was a soldier once, but served best as a medic! My hands were always better at healing than killing. If you still have a heart left…"

"Enough," Alexia snapped as she took a step forward. "If your hands are too soft, I'll do it myself."

Before Chiara could think, she moved. Her body betraying her training, placing itself squarely between Alexia's blades and Enan. Her own daggers came up, but not against Enan, against the *Dancer.*

Be careful, this one is good. I will come closer should you need me. Ness said, already knowing which way her mind had gone.

Alexia's eyes narrowed. Not surprise, not even anger, just a cold recognition as though she had seen this coming.

"Step aside," Alexia said. Her voice was soft now, a dangerous softness, like sand covering a pit of spikes.

Chiara swallowed. "He doesn't deserve to die."

"You don't decide," Alexia replied. "We do what the Empress commands. That is all."

From behind, Selene shifted, her hand clutching her own blades. "Chiara…" She said, almost pleading. "Don't make this worse."

But Chiara couldn't move. Her feet felt rooted, not by fear but by the certainty that if she stepped aside now, something in her would break beyond repair.

"No," she said. "Not like this."

"Then you've chosen your grave," Alexia said.

She struck without warning. Steel hissed through the air, her dagger flashing toward Chiara's ribs. Instinct screamed through Chiara's body. She parried, sparks kissing in the cramped air as blades clashed. The force of Alexia's strike rattled her wrist, and she staggered back, dragging Enan with her.

Selene cursed, stepping back to clear space, torn between them. Alexia pressed forward, daggers weaving in sharp, merciless arcs. She was faster, sharper, and overall just better than Chiara. Both *Dancers* knew it.

"You shame us all," Alexia spat between blows. "One weak heart will cost more than a hundred rebels. The Empress demands order, and you..." Steel slammed against steel, forcing Chiara to twist away "...you bring only chaos!"

Enan scrambled toward the far corner, clutching his arm to shield himself as the two *Dancers* blurred before him. Selene finally moved, her voice cutting across the clash. "Enough! Alexia, stop!"

But Alexia didn't stop. She drove harder, her daggers a flurry. Chiara caught one strike, twisted, and tried to rip the blade from Alexia's grip only to feel the flat of the second dagger slam against her temple.

Stars burst in her vision. She staggered, dropping to one knee.

Alexia moved in, walking past her. Enan reached for something, Chiara couldn't tell if it was a weapon or just the strap he'd been mending, and the room erupted.

Alexia's blade flashed, Enan dodged, and the table went over with a crash, bread and cheese scattering across the floor. Alexia came in from the side, but Enan was faster than she'd expected, grabbing a chair and swinging it hard. It caught Alexia across the shoulder, sending her back a step. The old man went sprinting out the backdoor they'd just come through as the two men from earlier came through the front.

"Alexia, get him. I'll deal with these two!" Selene shouted over the madness.

Chiara forced herself back to her feet and chased after Alexia. She knew Selene was more than capable of dealing with two hired hands. Besides, she'd not stepped in to defend her.

Enan was faster than she'd expected, and he knew the village. Chiara turned a corner trying to cut them off and found herself alone. She heard shouting to her left, and then a crash. Ahead, she spotted them. Alexia had cornered Enan against the side of a crumbling stall, her blades ready.

Ness! She shouted through her thoughts, hoping she was close enough to save the old man.

The jaguar exploded from the alley like lightning. Her coat gleamed gold in the sun, eyes like amber fire. Then, a sound like thunder as Ness roared before golden fur slammed into Alexia. She cried out once before being engulfed in a storm of claws and fangs.

There was a thudding of boots as Selene rounded the corner before freezing at the sight of the jaguar, blood dripping from its mouth, with one paw pinning the lifeless body of Alexia to the ground.

"Run, Enan." Chiara managed to muster the voice to say. He didn't need to be asked twice, disappearing down another alley.

There was a moment of stillness. Nothing moved or made a sound. Just the wind in the streets, the quiet thumping noise of blood dripping from fangs down to the ground. Selene took a solitary step forward, her eyes fixed on Ness, wide with horror. Gripping her blades tightly, Chiara stepped in between Ness and Selene.

"You brought a *Familiar*?" Selene hissed. "A soul-bonded beast? Are you mad?"

Chiara didn't have an answer, she just stared back at her.

Selene's face turned in an instant from that of fear, to utter revulsion. "You've betrayed everything the order stands for."

"She was going to kill me."

"She was right to. You let a target go. You endangered the mission, the order, and now you've brought that thing... that thing to murder one of our own?"

"Alexia was blinded by this creed. The Empress or whoever ordered this is wrong. He's not a rebel. This isn't a rebellion. Look around. These people are barely getting by."

"And now you're questioning the code. You're right, Chiara, Alexia would have killed you," Selene paused, reaching for her own daggers. "What makes you think I won't?"

"Because of her." She said as Ness let out a low grumbling roar and stepped past Chiara.

She has to die too, you know? If news gets back to the Pyramid...

"You really should go," Chiara said with finality. *She can make her own choices. I won't have her blood on my hands if I can help it.*

Fine, little one, but letting her go will bring only trouble our way.

"You're going to regret this, Chiara," Selene shouted before turning around and sprinting back out down the alley.

Chiara took a moment to recompose herself, letting her heart slow, and the pulsing in her brain to stop. She needed to think clearly, plan her next moves. Everything up until now had been foolish, she could no longer afford to be foolish. Alexia had seemed to know something was off about her from the start, why was she so perceptive? Her enchantment! That had to be it. The thought struck her like a bolt of lighting striking a dead tree in the dunes, the sparks almost jumped from her.

She slowly began to rifle through the dead *Dancers' robes* which were drenched in blood. A scrap of papyrus with Enan's likeness, an empty water skin and a single lion's fang was all she found.

She has a ring, that is the only personal effect I've seen any of you carrying. That must be it. Ness advised.

Of course the ring! Chiara cursed herself for not thinking of that before becoming covered in blood herself. *You have always been the brains of the two of us.*

I know, she purred.

A solitary golden, onyx ring shaped like a sleeping dragon with one red ruby eye was upon Alexia's left ring finger. Chiara gave a soft pull before, using her blade, cut away the finger and took off the ring, placing it on her right index finger. Her senses screamed instantly, as the light around her shone brighter, the grains of sand below appeared more sharp to see, and the way ahead seemed clearer.

We must go back to Vel Thassar and get Ramos out of there. The moment Selene reports what has happened here, the order will close ranks. They'll know of him, they must, and even anyone who has traded with me in the past will be eliminated. Poor Selene, she won't even realise she's signed her death warrant. Failure is final.

Then let us be gone. Ness grumbled her agreement.

THE HUNTER AND THE HUNTED

Chiara walked with her head low. Her hands would not stop trembling. The image of Selene's face, shock, then grief, then fury burned behind her eyes, replaying with every step she took. She would have to walk all the way back to Vel Thassar, because of course Selene had taken the horses. Had she really expected to be left one?

Ness padded beside her, silent but watchful, golden coat dulled to bronze in the fading light. The jaguar kept glancing back, ears twitching at sounds Chiara could not hear. Her heart hadn't slowed since making the decision to run back to Ramos, and since putting the ring on everything seemed heightened, the crack of stone underfoot, the hiss of wind through dry grass, the rasp of her own breath in her throat.

She told herself she had done what she had to. That Alexia would have cut her down if Ness hadn't intervened. That Selene had chosen to run rather than end it herself. She told herself many things, and none of them helped. She didn't know what was worse, that Alexia's death was on her hands, or that Enan's wasn't. He wasn't a rebel, he was just a poor farmer, but did that really matter? The Empress had ordered his death and she had defied that.

There was no going back now.

Her training said to shut it away, to harden herself against guilt. But the emptiness inside her did not feel like strength. It felt like she was hollowing out.

The sun dipped lower in the sky, a slow bleeding orb sinking into the horizon. Chiara adjusted the scarf around her face and pressed on, legs aching from the endless drag of sand. But with every mile her worry seemed to slowly engulf her more. If Selene went directly back to the Pyramid, the *Dancers* would find Ramos before she was even close to Vel Thassar and she'd arrive to find him... She forced the thought down before it could finish and picked up her pace.

By nightfall the desert had cooled, the dry heat of the day had bled away into a brittle chill. Shadows stretched long across the dunes, and all that was left was an eerie silence. Every sense Chiara had was currently firing off in her. She had learned long ago that the night belonged to the hunters. That usually meant her and Ness, but she wasn't so sure tonight.

We're not alone, Ness said with certainty. The jaguar's lean muscle tensed all over before she let out a low rumble of a growl. A vibration Chiara felt through the sand more than heard. The desert was not silent anymore.

She heard them now, the padding of paws against loose stone and sand, the whisper of the grass shifting even though there was no wind blowing. There was a flash of pale eyes in the dark, then another, before disappearing once again.

Lions, Chiara, stay close to me.

Her hands slid to her daggers out of instinct, though she knew the truth, the blades would be useless against a pride of them. Ness could kill one, maybe two, but there were more. Too many.

The first shape revealed itself on the crest of the dune ahead. It was a great brute of an animal, mane ragged, its shoulders rolling with a lazy strength. The beast stood in their path. Behind him, more shadows shifted, more eyes, more teeth.

"They're circling us," Chiara whispered. Her throat was as dry as the sand underfoot.

They test us, Ness replied, her voice sharp to Chiara's mind. *They want to see if we break.*

And by the Empress did she want to. Her body was screaming at her to run, any and all training had deserted her in this moment. But Ness was right, that would only drive them into a chase. Ness pressed close, her fur brushing Chiara's leg, anchoring them together. *Stand. Do not falter, they will not come unless they see weakness. Do not show them any.*

So she stood. Her knees shook, but she stood. She had her daggers loose in her grip, ready for them, though it was a poor comfort. The lions circled wider, their shapes weaving in and out of the half-light the moon was casting.

Growls rose and fell like the waves outside Ramos's house, constant. The minutes stretched into an hour, and then another until she felt herself swaying from both exhaustion and fear.

It was only when the eastern sky paled, and a faint bruise of violet and crimson illuminated the horizon, that the spell broke. One by one, the eyes blinked and turned away, their shapes melting back into the dunes. The ragged-maned brute of a lion gave a final snarl, then turned away himself.

Chiara's legs buckled, and she caught herself on Ness's flank. Her whole body trembled. "They could've taken us," she said hoarsely.

They did not. Ness shook herself, her golden fur catching the first rays of dawn. *And that is enough.*

She swallowed hard, forcing the spit down her throat and willed her feet to move again. Toward Vel Thassar, towards Ramos. Toward the answer to a question she feared, would he still be there when she arrived?

Chiara tasted it before she saw it, a bitter salty tang clinging to her lips. The dunes sloped lower, the grass thicker between them, the sea now visible in the distance.

Her body begged her to stop. Every step drove the heat deeper into her bones, the corners of her vision completely blurred into nothingness. She'd slept little since the lions. Her dreams were filled with Alexia's dead eyes, Selene's fury and the inescapable truth that she had broken every oath she had ever sworn.

By midmorning, the town had appeared, a sprawl of low stone houses on the coast, cluttered around its docks. The ships still swayed in the harbour, their masts dotting the horizon, it was as if nothing had changed. It was only when she got closer she realised everything had.

Overlooking the town she could see the bronze helms flashing in the streets. Soldiers. The gates were closed, dozens of spears gleamed above it. The town was locked down.

"You can't come in," Chiara whispered, brushing her hand over the warm curve of Ness's shoulder. "They'd see you well before we reached the walls."

I know.

"I'll come back," she promised. "Stay here, wait for me."

What else can I do? I'll see if there is any game around. Don't be too long, Ness replied, before lowering herself into the tall grass, vanishing.

Chiara drew her scarf tighter, pulled her hood low, and moved toward the walls where a crowd had begun forming, queuing to be let in. The patrols were sharp, but she was sharper. She let the noise of the crowd cloak her, as she slipped between merchants with baskets of fish, and ducked into alleys when soldiers turned their heads. The Black Pyramid had trained her well. Every step was thought about, every breath intended.

Still, her heart hammered in her chest like it was trying to break free. Each bronze cladded guard she passed felt like the edge of a blade skimming her throat. She finally reached Ramos's street, it felt familiar yet different. The shutters were closed, the doors bolted. The whole town seemed to hold its breath under the soldiers' watch. Her legs faltered slightly at the sight of his house, the door was still intact, as were the herbs still dying above its frame. They hadn't kicked his door down, that was a start at least. Chiara forced herself forward before knocking four times, in their own special way.

For a moment she was met with only silence, before there was a scrape of a bolt and the door creaked open a touch. Ramos's face appeared in the gap, tired, unshaven, but alive. His eyes widened at seeing her. "Chiara?"

Relief hit her so hard at that moment, that it broke her. Her knees gave way before she could stop them and the world tilted around her, blurring. She tried to speak his name but no sound came. She felt worry emanating from Ness before the darkness took her and she fell forwards.

A NECESSARY RETURN

Chiara woke to the sound of gulls. The first thing she felt was warmth, she was wrapped tightly under a blanket, a real blanket. It laid heavy over her, it was soft, not like the scratch of the desert, or the hard and coarse fabric of her cloak.

Beneath her was something much softer than the cold hard floor too, she was laid on a bed, a proper bed. It sagged beneath her with the use but it was soft, softer than anything she had slept on in days. Her body ached as though she had been trampled, her arms and legs felt incredibly stiff, her throat as raw and dry as she'd ever known it with every breath pulling against bruises she had no idea how she'd got.

The cries of the gulls circling the town, faint through the slats of the shuttered window, reminded her of where she was. Not the desert, but safely inside Vel Thassar, with Ramos.

You're alive, Ness purred into her mind.

You were worried?

Not at all, I actually quite enjoyed how light my thoughts were without your constant heavy presence.

What happened?

How should I know? One minute you were there, that itch in my thoughts, and the next gone. I tried to call to you a couple times but you had gone. I knew you hadn't died, I'd have known if that would have happened. Best to wake up now though, places to be, people to kill, you know?

Her eyes opened slowly, dragging against the sleep. She blinked them awake. The rafters above her head swam into focus, low and timbered, lit by the pale glow of daylight. There was the familiar smell of brine and herbs lingering in the air. She shifted slowly, biting down a hiss of pain and turned her head, wincing at the pull of her neck.

Ramos sat slouched in a chair by the window, back turned to her, resting his elbows on his knees. He was looking down through his clenched fingers at the floor, as if waiting for it to speak. His hair was a mess, his shirt was wrinkled, but he was there. He was alive. The relief hit her like a sudden wave and she simply had to close her eyes again.

The floor creaked as she shifted again. Ramos's head snapped up. For a heartbeat he simply stared at her, as if unsure she was real. Then he rose quickly, the chair scraping back.

"You're awake."

His voice was quiet, softer than she'd ever heard it before. She blinked against the sleep once more. He was at her side now, crouched low, studying her face in what appeared to be disbelief.

She wet her lips, and tried to speak, but only a rasp came out. "How long?"

"You've been out nearly two days," he said. "Barely breathing at first. I thought..." He broke off, staring absently at the wall behind her. "I thought I'd lost you."

Her eyes drifted shut. Two days gone. Ness must have waited, worrying at the edges of the town, unseen and alone. The thought pierced her sharper than any wound.

So that explains your mood, Chiara thought to Ness.

Well how would you react if I just disappeared without any warning for a few days? Ness replied.

You do! Often. How many times have you strayed from the den to hunt?

But I'm never not there! You know, like really there? You can always reach me, call to me. You just disappeared.

I know, I'm sorry. I must have just passed out.

Well, you're alive and you're safe. That's what matters.

"Are you okay?" Ramos asked, the concern was clear in his voice.

Her throat ached, the words that came out felt rough, but she forced them out anyways. "I'm here."

Ramos let out a slow breath, as though he'd been holding it all this time. "You shouldn't scare me like that," he said, trying to smile, but it faltered long before it reached his eyes.

Be kind to him. He's probably saved your life, Ness advised.

When am I not kind to him?

When are you? Ness scoffed.

"I didn't mean to," Chiara whispered to him.

"You never do," he said, lowering himself onto the edge of the cot, searching her face but for what, she wasn't sure. "Where were you, Chiara? What happened to you out there?"

It was the same question he always asked, just wrapped in a slightly different package. *Who are you, really?* She knew she couldn't tell him, not unless they were safely outside of Nadus. So, as always, she'd have to lie. She hated herself for it.

"I was travelling," she said, and then after a pause probably too long to be casual added. "It doesn't matter."

He frowned but let it lie, though the silence between them pressed heavily on her chest. She would have liked nothing more than to open her heart to him, to tell him all, to tell him about Ness. But she couldn't, not now. He leaned back slightly, rubbing at the scarred wood of the bedframe with his thumb.

He'll know me eventually, little one. He doesn't seem the type to let things lie. And I've seen enough of him to know him trustworthy. But for now you're right to shield him. Your kind could very well be on their way.

She pushed herself upright, propping her back against the wall. Every muscle within her screamed in protest, but the pain gave her something to focus her foggy mind on.

"What's happened here? Why all the guards?" She asked.

Ramos ran a hand through his hair. "Lockdown. The whole damn town. Started three nights ago, the day before you showed up at my door. A captain refused the new taxes on docking. I don't blame him, taxes seem to be going up with every cycle of the moon. Anyways, word spread quick, like it always does. A mob backed him, I nearly went out myself. Guards cut it down fast though. But not before half the docks where ablaze. Some idiot had taken it upon themselves to take a torch to the harbour master's office, like it's him who sets the taxes. The place went up like kindling."

He paused and walked over to the window, loosening the shutters so more light spilled into the room. "Since then, they've doubled the patrols. Anyone who so much as looks sideways at an officer, well, they drag 'em out in chains if they're feeling generous."

Chiara struggled to keep her focus. She sat straighter, ignoring the ache in her chest. If the lockdown wasn't because of her, then that settled it. Selene hadn't gone back to the Pyramid. Which meant, she was going to go back for Enan. She had to go back, to end it once and for all. If she didn't go back, Enan was as good as dead. She clenched her fists in the blanket. Her throat tightened. She almost spoke aloud, but stopped when Ramos's hand brushed hers.

"You're shaking," he said softly. "Here, drink."

He passed her a clay cup, water sloshing. She drank it greedily, though each swallow scraped raw against her throat. Still, it was clean, it was cool, it was refreshing. It was more than she deserved.

Ramos watched until she lowered the cup. Then he sighed whilst leaning back, gaze drifting back out the window back to the sea.

"You need rest. The streets are too dangerous right now. Half the folk are starving, the other half are desperate to flee. And…" He hesitated, then gave a short, strained laugh. "There's a ship for sale. Can you believe that? In the middle of this madness, a captain's selling off his boat for near nothing. By the Empress, it's a bargain, Chiara. If I had the coin…"

His voice trailed off at that, and something old and familiar returned to his face. That wistful longing she knew so well from him, the dream of the west, of the Old Empire, of escape. Coin, coin was always the issue.

"But?" She asked quietly.

Ramos's eyes had dimmed almost as quickly as they'd brightened. "But it's not cheap enough. Even if I sold the house, the nets, everything. I still wouldn't have enough for the ship, and a crew. And what good's a ship without hands to deck her right?"

Chiara stared at him, the words gathering in her throat but refusing to leave her mouth. She thought of Alexia's lifeless eyes, of the blood on her hands, of the value of the ring she had taken. A mark of a true *Dagger Dancer*. Her path had already broken. There was no returning to the Pyramid now. The ring was merely a symbol of what she could never return to.

Slowly, she reached for the pouch at her belt, still lying on the chair beside the bed. Her fingers closed around the cool metal of the ring. She drew it out, held it up in the morning light. The gold was unmistakeable, gleaming faintly even through the grime and blood and dust.

Ramos's eyes widened. "Where in the Empress's name did you…"

"Take it," she said, pressing it into his palm before she could think better of it.

"Chiara."

"It's not what you think," Chiara said quickly. She held his hand steady, curling his fingers around it. "It's not real. A fake trinket, meant to look like an enchanted relic, but it isn't. Just gold. Worth enough to buy your ship. And a crew."

"Chiara…" Ramos started again.

"Sell it," she cut in, her voice harder than she meant it to be. "It's enough to make the dream real. Get the ship. Just be ready."

"For what?" His eyes lifted to hers, confusion and desperation tangled there.

She held his gaze. "For me. When I come back, we'll sail west. Together."

"Chiara, you're not going anywhere, you were on death's door not two days ago."

She reached up, wrapping her arms around his neck and pulled him in for a kiss. She felt the warmth of his lips on hers immediately, and the fluttering of her heart. She pulled away, and began to get up.

"I have to go. One final time, I can't tell you where. But this time is the last. If I'm not back within the week, go without me."

"I couldn't!" He protested.

"But you must, promise me."

"Why?"

"Just do it."

"If you're not back within the week, I'll set sail," he paused with a gulp. "Without you."

"Good. When we next see each other, I'm looking forward to introducing you to a good friend of mine. I think you'll like her very much."

Who doesn't?

TO PREPARE FOR A DANCER

The desert gave them little respite on the way back. Ness padded beside her in silence. Her golden coat was dulled by the dust and sand. They walked in comfortable silence at first. The road north and west wound low through the dry scrub, the horizon shivering with the heat. Every dune looked the same, every step like the last. The hours seemed to blur into each other.

You couldn't have stayed with him, as much as you would have liked to, Ness said finally. *The man would have kept you safe though, and fed.*

Why is it always food with you?

What else is there to think about?

Chiara shook her head. *You're right though, as always. Selene won't stop. She won't stop with just Enan. Every villager there is a loose end, and she'll want to tidy it all up before returning to the sisters.*

She might yet kill you, have you thought about that?

The thought cut through her like the rising wind. Chiara pushed on, tightening her grip on her cloak. "Then at least I tried," she said aloud.

Ness gave a low rumble in response. *Stubborn cub.*

By late afternoon the outline of the village rose from

the haze. Low mud brick homes, smoke curling from chimneys, goats grazing in the thin grass beyond the pens. To any other traveller it was nothing, a forgotten corner of Nadus. But to the Pyramid, to the *Dancers*, it was a nest of rebellion, a sickness to be cut out before it spread. For Chiara, it looked like redemption. There was no rebellion here, just hungry farmers and a dead *Dancer*. Selene wouldn't care though.

We'll go in together. If Selene isn't already here, you hide. The first thing she'll do is look for you, she won't want to fight me with the chance of you pouncing from the shadows.

She won't have a choice, Chiara.

They slipped around the outer edge of the village and entered by a narrow lane where children were playing in the dust. Their laughter stuttered into silence as Ness passed. Wide eyes followed them, and one boy ran off, shouting for his mother.

Chiara pulled her hood lower. She knew what it looked like, an armed stranger with a great beast at her side. It wasn't the most welcoming of looks, and she couldn't afford spooking Enan. If he ran again, if he hid before she could speak to him, then this was all ruined. If he was still alive.

She crossed the village slowly, watching for signs of Selene's passing. Any markings, guards, unusual movement. But there was nothing. Just a few children

61

chasing a piglet, and a woman arguing with her husband near a rope line hung with drying clothes. Eventually, she found him.

Enan was sitting at a low table outside of the house they had accosted him in before. A different pair of men stood nearby, thick-shouldered and bearded, holding cudgels the length of walking sticks. They wore brown tunics and leather belts. Not soldiers this time. Just farmers with sticks.

Enan saw her and stood immediately.

"You," he said, a grin spreading across his face. "By the sands, you made it."

Chiara dipped her head. "You're alive. I wasn't sure I'd be here in time."

He stepped forward, arms slightly open, but stopped short when Ness padded up behind her and growled low. His eyes widened. "Is that... a cat?"

"She's not here for you," Chiara said tersely.

He raised his hands. "Right. Sorry. Didn't mean anything."

The two men behind him tensed but didn't move.

"I thought you were dead," Enan said.

The men with the clubs watched her carefully.

"Friends of yours?" She asked.

"My cousins. Evra and Reel. They think I'm important now."

"Are you?"

He hesitated. "Not… exactly. Let's talk inside. Come on, there's room for your friend."

Enan stepped aside quickly, ushering them in. Three villagers sat against the wall, one with his arm bound in fresh cloth, another with a cough that rattled like stones in a jar. They stared at Chiara and Ness with open suspicion, but Enan waved them out.

When the room was clear, he sagged into a chair and rubbed his eyes. "You saved me, dancer. I don't know why. I've seen your kind work. You don't hesitate."

Chiara felt the sting of his words, but she forced herself to answer. "I couldn't do it. You're not a rebel."

"No." His smile was bitter. "Not a rebel. Just a farmer trying to keep his people fed. The levy went up this season. Twice what we gave last year. We couldn't pay. So we hid a little grain each harvest. Enough to survive. Enough to keep our children alive."

Chiara swallowed. She had expected something like this, but hearing it out loud pressed harder than she'd thought it would.

Enan leaned back, his gaze distant. "That was all it took to send three *Dancers*? I didn't know the collectors had even realised they were missing anything. No soldiers have been sent, no demands made. Surely this has to be about something else. I heal the sick here, I set bones, I help where I can. So they see me as some sort of leader. I never asked for it."

"The Empress hates mess. Taxes beget order, order beget prosperity. Or so I've been told, many times. You are a mess, one that needs cleaning up, even more so after my interference."

He glanced at Ness. "That cat's really something."

At least someone notices, Ness purred.

"She is." Chiara glanced at Ness. The jaguar's eyes glowed faintly in the dim light. "You know they'll send her again."

Enan nodded. The two men from before entered, as if on cue. Broad shouldered, carrying clubs. They looked at Chiara with thinly veiled distrust. Enan gestured to them. "My cousins. They'll protect me, should it come to it."

Chiara studied them, the way their grips shifted uneasily on the wood, the way their eyes darted toward Ness. Farmers, not fighters. Brave, maybe. But bravery wouldn't last long against a trained *Dancer*.

"You had friends before, trained friends, and Selene killed them."

"There are more than just these two, the village will not allow for unseen entrants again."

"There is one thing I've been meaning to ask you. When we came last time, through that back door there, before we entered we saw a figure exit, with purple eyes."

Enan looked confused, and a little scared. "There had been no one that I was aware of in this house until you had entered it."

He's not lying, you can tell, he looks afraid. Afraid, because he knows you're not lying either.

She said nothing. Sighing, she pulled a stool closer and sat, the dagger at her belt heavy against her side.

"You're welcome to make yourself at home, I assume you wish to stay for a while? If you don't mind me I have a couple things to attend to. Please, do make yourself comfortable," Enan said with clearly as much bravery as he could muster before scurrying out of the room, closely followed by the two club-wielding men.

For a moment, Chiara let herself imagine the village as it might have been, quiet, ordinary, unremarkable. The kind of place no *Dancer* should ever have touched. But she knew better than to trust those moments. Selene would come. It was only a matter of when.

Night fell heavy over the village. The air cooled, but Chiara's skin still burned from the sun. She sat outside Enan's home, cloak pulled tight, Ness curled low beside her. The jaguar's slow breaths blended with the steady hum of crickets. Inside, Enan spoke quietly with his cousins. Their voices rose and fell, muffled by the mud brick walls, the words lost but the worry plain enough. Chiara did not need to hear them to know what they said. Plans for a defence. Hopes that dawn would come without blood.

She looked toward the horizon instead. Every flicker of a shadow, every shape that moved in the dark grass, she measured against the thought of Selene. She half expected to see her even now, daggers gleaming.

You should sleep, Ness murmured, eyes still closed. *Your body is weak.*

"I can't," Chiara whispered.

Then at least eat.

Chiara almost smiled at that. Ness had hunted earlier, slinking out into the scrub and returning with a small hog. She had pushed the meat toward Chiara, as though her own hunger meant nothing. Chiara had eaten a little, but not enough. She let her head fall back against the wall, eyes closing. The night was too quiet.

The door creaked open. Enan stepped out, his shadow falling across the dirt. He lowered himself onto the ground a short distance from her. For a while, he said nothing.

"You're not what I expected," he said at last.

Chiara opened her eyes. "What did you expect?"

He shrugged, his gaze set on the stars above. "A ghost, maybe. The kind that kills in silence, leaves without a trace. That's what the dancers are to us. Not... this." He gestured toward her, his expression unreadable. "Not someone who hesitates."

Chiara felt her throat tighten. "Maybe I shouldn't have."

"Maybe," Enan agreed. "But if you had, there'd be no one left to tend the children's fevers. No one to mend a broken leg when the ox stumbles. No one to speak when the others are too afraid. So forgive me if I don't curse your hesitation.

"My cousins will fight for me," Enan said, softer now. "But they're not warriors. They've never had to kill."

Chiara glanced toward the house. Enan wasn't wrong, they appeared willing enough, but trained killers they were not.

Enan followed her gaze, then smiled. "You don't think much of them."

"They're brave," Chiara said carefully.

He chuckled. "Brave is only the word we use when men are too foolish to know fear." His smile faded. "Still. Brave or foolish, they are what I have."

"You're wrong," she replied. "You can only truly be brave, when you are afraid."

"Poetic. A killer and a poet, there is no end to the amazements," he mused. "There are stories told here of a purple eyed wizard. It's a children's story, a scary one. He doesn't really exist. I don't know what you saw, but if it was him, then I really am in trouble."

"And what does the story tell of him?"

"That he is the most powerful being in Nadus, the Empress be damned. That he controls the lions, and they do his bidding. That he can see through them, that he watches through them. The tales change from person to person, but that's the gist of it."

"Interesting."

Finally, Enan asked, "Why did you come back?"

Chiara shifted, feeling Ness stir against her leg. "Because Selene will."

"And you'll stop her?"

"I'll try."

Enan studied her for a long moment. "Then may the gods keep your hands quick."

He rose then, brushing dust from his robe, and returned inside.

He trusts you, Ness whispered, head lifting slightly.

He shouldn't.

But he does.

The night passed without movement, but rest never came. Every sound pulled Chiara's eyes open, every rustle of grass set her hand on her blades. When dawn broke, her body felt as stiff as stone.

SWORN TO PROTECT

The village stirred with the sun. Women drew water from the well, men shouldered baskets, children darted between houses. They looked at Chiara and Ness with the wary curiosity of those who did not know whether to fear or thank them.

Enan emerged, his face looked tired but calm. He greeted the villagers, spoke with them, touched their shoulders, offered a word here and there. Chiara watched him, and for the first time she believed him when he said he had not asked to lead. He had become one by necessity, by kindness mistaken for defiance.

By midmorning, the cousins returned from the fields, clubs resting against their shoulders. Their eyes strayed frequently towards the road that led east. "Theres no sign of…" they began before a scream from the far edge of the village rang through the air.

Chiara found herself moving before thinking. She raced past the well, down the muddy path lined with crooked fences and sleeping goats. Her boots pounded the dirt. Ness followed like a streak of flame through the streets.

Ahead a figure appeared, at first just a blur of black fabrics. Selene. She stepped into view like smoke taking shape, her cloak torn and stained with dried blood. Her hair was loose, wet with sweat, framing her pale, beautiful face. Her eyes locked onto Chiara's and she smiled.

The cousins stepped in front of her, taking a couple of steps towards the *Dancer*.

"Get back," she snapped, but they ignored her.

Selene stopped her approach merely ten paces away.

"Run," Chiara hissed. "Now."

"Have you seen the size of her? And she doesn't have some beast like you," Evra said.

Reel raised his club.

"No," Chiara said, louder. "Don't…"

Her protest was cut off by his shouts as he charged. It was over in a breath.

Selene moved like water, twisting around his blow, and slicing his throat open with a blade Chiara hadn't seen drawn. Blood sprayed across the dirt. Reel collapsed to the floor hard, his last few desperate breaths gurgling in the dirt.

Evra looked dumbfounded for a second, before roaring himself and running forward directly at Selene. She turned and drove her curved dagger into his chest, twisting it hard, and with a strength that defied her size lifted him off the ground before tossing him aside like a sack of grain. Both of the men were dead in under five seconds. She had tried to warn them. Chiara didn't move, Ness crouched low next to her, growling. Selene looked up at her, blood dripping from both hands.

"Such a shame, another two dead," she said softly. "Because of you."

"Leave the village. I'm the one you want."

"You think you know what I want? Traitor," Selene hissed the word.

Still, Chiara didn't move. She let the word settle in the air between them.

Selene stepped over one of the corpses, her twin daggers drawn, their obsidian blades humming faintly in the heat. "You lied to us. You let Alexia die. You've sided with them."

"I saved Enan's life because he isn't who you think he is," Chiara said, voice low, calm despite the thundering beat of her heart. "They're not rebels. They're farmers trying to survive."

"Farmers don't take up arms against the Capital. They don't hide in the desert like rats. They don't…"

"They do," Chiara cut in, stepping forward now, her own daggers sliding free. "When the alternative is starvation."

Selene's lip curled. "You think you know better than the Council? Than our sisters? You dishonour all of us by standing here."

"If that's how you see it, so be it."

Selene stopped five feet away. Her expression was cold. Grieving. Furious. Her face, once so perfect, so composed, was cracked now with sorrow and rage. "You betrayed your sisters," she said. "You betrayed your vow. You betrayed me."

Chiara said nothing. She knew Selene would not be dissuaded. This was already written, there was no argument, no plea, no truth that could change the course of what was to come.

Selene flashed a predatory smile. "Your little pet won't save you this time."

And she's going to stop me? Ness scoffed.

With a flash of green her dagger ignited, before a ball of flames flew in their direction forcing them to dive in opposite directions. Ness dived into the next alley, but the flames destroyed a stall next to them and blocked her in.

Don't die, I'll find a way around.

Selene struck first. She moved like a storm, daggers flashing, feet gliding across the sand. Chiara barely brought her blades up in time, parrying two rapid slashes meant for her throat. Their blades kissed, scraped, and shrieked in the hot air. The heat from Selene's dagger was unnaturally hot, as their blades pressed together she could feel her own begin to melt away.

Chiara stepped back, pivoting, trying to find a rhythm. Selene pressed, relentlessly. She quickly parried a slash to her ribs, then spun away from a lunge to her thigh. Taking yet another step back she blocked away a stab aimed for her throat. She had no choice but to play defence, Selene was attacking with a primal fury and for now she had no way of stemming the tide. Selene spun round and Chiara thought she might have her own opening, so lunged only to be met with Selene's heel digging under her ribs. She was flung backwards from the impact, the breath driven from her lungs. She hit the floor hard on her back, but forced her body to roll over. She struggled back to her feet. They circled one another, breathless.

"You could have been one of us," Selene said, slicing low. Chiara jumped back. "You were my friend!"

"I still am," Chiara snapped. "You're just too blind to see it."

Selene feinted right and then turned left, blade sweeping for Chiara's shoulder. Chiara dropped, ducking below the blow, and slashed across Selene's thigh. Her blade bit flesh, earning her a spray of blood which wet the sands beneath them.

Selene staggered, but only for a moment. Her anger flared, and she came forward harder than before. Chiara barely blocked the next flurry. She twisted, slashing Selene's forearm. Selene cursed and spun, her dagger catching Chiara's wrist. Metal met skin, and a searing hot sensation flew up her arm. Chiara hissed in pain and dropped one of her blades, her right hand suddenly useless.

Selene grinned. "You're slowing."

Chiara could only grunt in response. She shifted her remaining dagger in her left hand and tightened her grip. Selene rushed again. Chiara stepped aside and landed a desperate jab toward Selene's ribs, grazing her, but Selene grabbed her wrist and drove her knee into Chiara's stomach. The wind fled Chiara's lungs for a second time. She collapsed to one knee, gasping. Selene didn't pause, the kick landed hard across Chiara's jaw, sending her skidding across the courtyard, her remaining dagger spinning from her grasp as the world spun around her.

Chiara coughed, blood falling from her lips and nose. She scrambled on the sand, reaching for her weapon, but Selene was already on her.

"Goodbye, sister," she whispered.

She raised both blades high and Chiara closed her eyes. So this was it, how she would die. She hadn't even saved Enan. But she was brave enough to try, and perhaps in a strange way, that was what mattered most.

The world roared around her, there was a blur of golden fur and a terrified scream from Selene. Ness slammed into her like a boulder falling from the sky. The jaguar's body smashed Selene to the ground, claws ripping across her ribs, fangs snapping for her throat. The force of the blow knocked both of them aside. Selene thrust one dagger up blindly, its inflamed steel plunged into Ness's side. The jaguar shrieked, blood gushing from her wound.

Chiara crawled toward her dropped dagger. Her hand closed around it just as Selene, bleeding from half a dozen wounds and pinned beneath the jaguar, tried to rise. Selene's hand reached for the other dagger.

Chiara screamed and lunged. With both hands on the hilt, ignoring the pain flaring up her injured wrist, she drove the dagger deep into Selene's throat. Selene's eyes widened. Her lips moved, trying to speak, but only blood came out. She slumped beneath Ness, body limp.

Chiara rolled away, panting, staring at the sky. Her arms trembled, her body sticky with sweat, sand, and blood. Ness whimpered softly, the dagger still embedded in her ribs.

It was a good fight. A good hunt. A worthy prey.

Chiara pushed herself to her knees, crawled toward her.

"Hold on," she whispered. "Stay with me."

Ness blinked slowly, blood pooling around her. Her sides heaved with each breath.

Chiara placed her hand on the great cat's flank and pressed gently, trying to slow the bleeding. But it was bad. The blade had gone deep, far deeper than it should have. The magical flames had allowed it cut through both flesh and bone and now it was stuck.

She looked at Selene's body, her fallen sister. Her eyes were still open, the expression frozen somewhere between fury and disbelief.

Chiara whispered a quiet blessing to honour dead *Dancers*. "May your spirit find the veil, Selene."

Then she turned back to Ness, tears mixing with the dust on her face.

"I'm going to get us out of here."

Get yourself out. Go. Go meet Ramos and find this Empire of his.

"Not without you, old friend."

I fear I am not long for this plane. I go to the great hunt in the sky with the rest of my kind.

"No, not yet you don't," Chiara cried, burying her head into Ness's neck.

Someone's coming, Ness warned.

Only then did Chiara hear footsteps. She turned, one arm shielding Ness.

Enan emerged from behind the low stone dwelling, his arms raised to show he bore no weapon. "You alright?" he asked.

Chiara didn't answer. She was watching Ness's side, the blood still leaking out with each laboured breath. Ness growled faintly.

Enan crouched beside her. "She's not just a pet."

"No," Chiara said, her voice pained. "She's family."

Enan studied the great cat for a moment, then stood abruptly. "Wait here."

He disappeared into one of the buildings. Chiara stroked Ness's head with her uninjured hand, she could see Ness fading, the rise and fall of her chest growing slower, the heat from her body dimming. Enan returned moments later, holding a cloth-wrapped object in both hands. Carefully, reverently, he knelt and began to unwrap it.

Inside was a bracelet. It was bronze, and unassuming.

The very opposite of the ring she'd given to Ramos. The metal had strange vinework etched into it, fine, looping thorns climbing around the gem like ivy. All Chiara could do was stare.

"This was my father's," Enan said. "He used it during the border wars, years ago. He was a field medic. They say it was forged in the Capital. A gift from a princess to a doctor. I don't really know. All I can say for certain is it made me a very popular man when I served my time as a medic."

"What does it do?" she asked, already knowing.

"Healing," Enan said. "Not instantly, but enough. If the patient is still alive, if the heart hasn't stopped, it'll start the body back on its path."

He reached toward Ness. Chiara grabbed his wrist. "Careful."

He nodded. "May I?"

She hesitated, then let go.

Enan slipped the bracelet onto his wrist, then placed his palm gently on Ness's side, just beside the dagger. The bronze glowed faintly, like sunlight under water. Enan winced, Chiara saw his body tense, as if something had drawn from him. And then, Ness stirred.

It wasn't a leap or a lunge, but her breathing shifted, it became stronger. Her eyes focused more fully. Her tail twitched. The object pulsed with that same quiet green light that Selene's dagger had. Enan didn't move his hand.

"It's working," Chiara whispered, her throat tight.

"She's still bleeding," he said. "I can only do so much. Pull the blade. Slowly."

Chiara bit her lip and braced her hand against Ness's flank. "I'm sorry," she whispered, and drew the dagger free.

Ness let out a guttural snarl, nothing that she could understand, but she didn't thrash. Her claws dug into the ground. Blood gushed for a moment, Chiara pressed a cloth against it as Enan moved his hand again, now over the open wound.

The green light swirled, dimming, then pulsed stronger. Over the next minute, the gaping wound began to close. First the deeper tissue knit, then the outer flesh puckered and sealed. When the light finally faded, the wound was still raw, pink, and clearly painful, but it was closed. Stitched by magic.

Ness's breathing slowed. Her head settled against Chiara's knee.

"She'll need rest," Enan said, standing. His voice was hoarse. "But she'll live."

Chiara bowed her head. "Thank you."

Enan nodded and looked toward Selene's corpse. "That one came to kill me?"

"Yes."

"But not because of rebellion. I'm no rebel."

Chiara shook her head. "You were never a rebel. I knew

the moment you started talking about tax hikes and irrigation ditches."

"So why did she come?" he asked, voice low.

Chiara glanced down at the bracelet still on his wrist. "Because of that."

Enan frowned.

"She was one of ours," Chiara said. " Dancers don't get sent to kill farmers. They get sent to kill threats. Someone in the Capital knows you have that thing. And they think it shouldn't be out here."

Enan stared at the band, twisting it slowly. "It saved dozens of lives in the war. My father refused to give it up. Said magic like this shouldn't belong to kings and killers. It should be used to save."

"They disagree."

He sighed and slipped it off, offering it back to her. "You take it."

Chiara stared at the band. "No."

"You'll need it," Enan said. "That wound on your wrist needs tending. And that jaguar isn't out of danger."

"I can't take your inheritance."

Enan gave her a wry smile. "Would you rather I die with it on my hand when they send the next someone?"

Chiara hesitated, then took it. The metal was warm from his skin. She turned it in her hand before slipping it into a pouch on her belt. She looked over to where Selene had fallen.

She had carried two packs with her. One was light, probably containing food and water. The other was heavier. Chiara opened both, checking quickly. Rations, a waterskin, medical salves. Coins too, more than a *Dancer* would usually carry. What was she meaning to do with those? Possibly run, she must have known then, that the moment she went back to the Pyramid her life was forfeit.

Enan picked up the dagger, and allowed it to glow green for a second before dousing it. "She was a friend of yours?" He asked.

Chiara closed the pack. "She was more than that. She was my sister."

"I'm sorry."

Chiara slung the pack over her shoulder and crouched beside Ness. The jaguar opened one eye and gave a low grumble. "We're leaving," Chiara said gently. "We'll find shade soon."

I will try. Though you may need to be our guardian for a little while.

Enan stepped closer. "Will you come back?"

"No, I do not believe I will."

"Then I may need to become the rebel they think me to be." He chuckled looking down at the dagger.

"What will you do?"

"I don't really know. Perhaps take whoever can go, and make a run for the forest. I hear it's cool there, with plenty of fresh water. Can you imagine it? A life with no sand."

"You're not a rebel, Enan," she said. "But maybe that's exactly why they want you gone."

He didn't answer.

"Do you have a way for me to send a message?"

To that, he only smiled.

THE NEW AND OLD WORLD

The hawk had flown swift and true. Enan had called her Iyra, an old, lean bird with clever eyes and a speckled breast. Chiara had tied the message to her leg with steady fingers, whispering to her softly before sending her skyward. Iyra had wheeled once, twice, then vanished southward over the dunes.

Now Chiara stood barefoot in the sand at Vel Theror, the sea breeze tugging at her sleeves. The village lay behind her, little more than a scattering of clay homes and net-laden poles. A fishing town much smaller than Vel Thassar. It was quiet, unremarkable, and precisely what she needed.

Before her, the sea stretched out like hammered silver, the horizon hazy with heat and salt. Ness lay nearby, curled in the shade of a low rocky outcrop. Her fur still bore the signs of her wound, matted and dark, but she breathed easier now. Her golden eyes watched the waves.

Chiara sank into the sand beside her.

"Remember this place?" she asked.

Ness blinked slowly. *We came here when I was just a cub.*

"Yes! We camped here once," Chiara said, "before I was even a proper initiate. I snuck off to swim. You tried to

82

catch a crab and got pinched on the nose."

That crab still ended up as dinner, as I recall. Ness rumbled faintly in the way she did when she laughed.

They sat in silence for a while. The wind hissed down from across the dunes. Gulls circled lazily overhead, and somewhere behind the village, a bell tolled for noon. Chiara leaned back and stretched her legs.

"I don't know what's waiting for us across the sea," she said at last. "Ramos says the Empire's ruins still breathe. That there are cities swallowed by vines and old palaces half-sunk in the jungle. Magic, he says, even older than the Pyramid."

There's nothing older than the Pyramid. It's part of the land, your people have only moved into it. Ness snorted.

"I know," Chiara said. "He's a liar."

But the lie had hope in it. That was the part Chiara clung to. A life free from the oppressive sands and heat of Nadus. A life free from the *Dancers*. A life where she could be free from forever looking over her shoulder, free from wondering if tonight was the night a blade would find itself in her back.

She watched the sea for hours, drifting in and out of sleep. When she opened her eyes again, the sun had begun to dip, and there, on the horizon, cutting through the haze like a knife, was a sail.

She stood at once. "He came."

The sail was dark red, faded, and completely

unfamiliar. But it had to be him. There was no reason for a ship of that size to be anywhere near here.

So begins the start of our next adventure.

"So it does. No more *Dancers*. No more rebels. No more lies. I can be me, he can be him and you can be you."

Ness rose shakily and padded to her side. Together they watched the ship draw closer, its wide belly parting the waves. As it neared the reef, it slowed, and Chiara saw the figures moving along the deck, shouting, pointing, adjusting the ropes.

She dragged the small rowboat from its hiding place and pushed it into the surf. "Come on, you big scaredy cat."

Ness hesitated, then, at Chiara's soft teasing, leapt in. The boat rocked, nearly tipping, but settled. Chiara rowed. The sea was calm, which made rowing easy. The ship's shadow loomed above them before long, and a thick rope ladder was tossed down. Voices called out from above.

"Chiara?"

"Is that...? By the Empress, that is her!"

Chiara slung her pack over her shoulder and gripped the ladder. The crew lowered a wide sling to gently haul Ness aboard first.

Am I supposed to be lifted in that? No, not a chance.

"Would you rather swim back?" Chiara asked.

I see your point, she growled, but clung to the ropes

anyway as the net lifted her. Chiara followed, climbing hand over hand until she hauled herself onto the deck. A dozen sailors stood in stunned silence, staring at Ness, who paced in a wide circle around the mast before collapsing with a dramatic huff.

It's like they've never seen a jaguar before, Ness chuckled.

She let out a quiet laugh, and dusted herself off before looking up. "Ramos," Chiara said.

He stepped from the quarterdeck. His coat was sunbleached, his eyes rimmed with exhaustion, but the smile he gave her was unmistakable. The pure joy that coursed through her at that moment was indescribable. The weight and worry from the past week vanished into his deep brown eyes.

"I knew you'd make it," he said.

She walked to him, and for a moment they simply just looked at each other.

"You look different," he said at last.

"I am different," she said.

His gaze drifted to Ness. "You were hiding her this whole time?"

Chiara smiled faintly. "Her secret wasn't mine to reveal."

Ramos grinned at her in response before shouting over her shoulder, "What are you standing around for, back to it!"

The crew had begun to move again, men began to pull the ropes tighter, and the sails got adjusted. Ramos led her toward the bow, away from prying ears.

"Everything went to hell after you vanished," he said. "The Black Pyramid is in lockdown. Rumors everywhere. They say a dancer went rogue. There have been reports of three other towns in full, open rebellion. The whole Empire's gone to shit. We've picked the right time to be out."

"I suppose I did."

He looked at her sidelong. "You killed someone."

"I killed a sister."

"You were a dancer all this time, with a golden jaguar, a creature of myth by your side. Is there anything else you haven't told me? Is your name really Chiara?"

"Well…" She paused, enjoying the incredulous look on his face. "My name is Chiara, I didn't lie about that, or about my love for you."

"I think that's the first time you've said that."

"No, surely not."

"Yes, it is, I would remember you saying it. I love you too, Chiara."

She reached out and grabbed his hand, lacing her fingers through his. Wind lashed her hair. Behind them, the shores of Nadus shrank, its craggy cliffs and golden sands fading into both the distance and memory. She wouldn't be coming back, that much she knew.

Ramos leaned on the railing beside her. "There's a place I've heard about," he said after a while. "An old river city deep in the jungle. Will take a day or two from the shore to reach it. But the bones of the Old Empire run beneath it, aqueducts, vaults, even a shattered throne supposedly."

"A throne?"

"I thought you might like a seat," he said with a grin.

Chiara looked out at the sea, a smile forming on her face. "You once asked me what I do," she said.

Ramos nodded. "I remember."

She turned to face him. "I don't do anything anymore," she said. "I was the last true dagger dancer. The protector of the people. I protected the weak, from those who sought to do them harm, and in doing so have broken every vow I ever made."

Ramos studied her, then nodded. "I think you still are. A protector," he said quietly.

The sails caught the wind and the ship tilted forward, carving a path into the wide blue beyond. Behind them, Nadus burned in the sun, an empire of sand and secrets and blood, and it grew smaller with every wave. Chiara didn't look back.

JUST THE BEGINNING

Long after dusk, Chiara stood at the stern, Ness curled beside her in a coil of sailcloth. The stars were bright tonight, millions of cold lights flickering above the endless black sea.

She looked down at her opened hand. In her palm lay a single piece of obsidian. It was a piece of rubble that her and Selene had picked from the Pyramid in their first weeks there. The same stone Selene had carried in her boot all those years. Chiara closed her fingers around it, pressed it to her heart, and then cast it into the waves. The ship sailed on. An empire awaited.

THANK YOU FOR READING

To all of those who have made it this far, I would like to say thank you. You have taken the time to read this book and for that, I am forever grateful.

If you could take the time, to leave a review on a platform of your choice that would be incredibly supportive. As a self published author, reviews really do help in persuading other readers to take a chance on my book.

Writing is an escape for me. An escape from the dreary monotony of adult life. To think that I get to share that escape now with so many of you is honestly something I cannot fully comprehend.

Thank you - Callum Rushworth

Turn the page for a sneak preview of

THE SUMMONER

PROLOGUE

It had been a massacre. There they laid, dead or dying. Some of the finest knights the kingdom of Veridia had ever seen. They lay there, riddled with bolts, strewn across the side of the road akin to a hunted boar. These honourable men could have held his throne room for an eternity, instead they lie there now, discarded, like common criminals.

"He did tell you to come alone." A cloaked figure ahead of him chided, snapping Lucian out of his daze.

Three identical cloaked figures stood side by side ahead of him, wickedly curved blades hanging casually by their sides. Above them on the crumbling stone walls of what must have once been a gatehouse stood a dozen or so more cloaked figures, crossbows pointed at him.

"What the fuck is this?" Lucian demanded indignantly, taking a step towards his assailants and unsheathing his sword.

The cloaked figure in the middle, the one who had spoken before, raised their blade and pointed it at him. Their unnatural purple eyes glowed hot."No. No, no, no. Just no. You really do not want to do that."

"He said he would help me! He said he was a friend,

and now he has you murder my men?" Lucian exclaimed, taking another step forward.

"He really did tell you to come alone, he does not like to be ignored." The figure replied coolly.

"But I am the King! I do not obey, I am obeyed!" He shouted across to them all.

"You *were* the King, isn't that why you're here? To regain your power, to retake your throne? To have the ability to depose the usurper, and once more possess your birthright?" The words were sharper than the steel he held, cutting him to the bone. He stopped in his tracks. The figure ahead smiled.

"Good, if that is still the case, now we have unburdened you of your chaperones, we can take you to him. But let us get one thing clear from the outset, *King* Lucian. You need him, he does not need you. He has summoned you, for reasons only he knows. Should you choose to ignore his commands any further, we will be happy to leave you like your men. Am I understood?"

"Shit," was all Lucian could muster in response, sheathing his sword. The man had bristled him, and stung his pride. The stranger had summoned him? Lucian thought. No, he had requested his presence. He was a king, not a dog to come running obediently when called. There was no use arguing now though, these zealots may just kill him if he did.

"Very good. Then we may begin. Follow me, we will

escort you the rest of the way." The figure spoke, before turning curtly and walking through the remnants of the gate, quickly followed by the other two. Lucian hurried to catch up, glancing upwards to the crumbling stone where the other figures had been, now seemingly vanished.

"Who are you? Are you his followers?" Lucian asked, hoping to understand more of his mysterious supposed ally.

"My name is of no significance, *your grace*. I am merely your guide. Followers may be a word you could describe us as, our order is much more than that though. You will learn more soon enough, should he choose to enlighten you." Everytime the figure referred to his true monarch title, the words were laced with acid, like he was mocking him. It unsettled Lucian. They walked on for what felt like an age. After walking through the gates, the land became increasingly steeper as the large Volcano Pyrepeak loomed above in the distance.

Trudging up through the rugged terrain, his weathered boots crunched in the ashen laid ground which had settled like snow. The air, hazy with fine dust, tickled the back of his throat. His breath came in sharp short gasps, more laborious as the path got harder and higher. The mix of coarse fabrics and leather, barely shielded him from the ash and the occasional gusts of wind. The three figures ahead seemed undaunted by the elements, traversing easily up the rocks. Pyrepeak became closer and closer with every tired step he took. The world around him was soon alive with fire and brimstone. Lucian had left familiar landscapes of civilization behind a long time ago, given way to the bare, ruined landscape of this volcanic wasteland. He was tired, damn tired. The escape through the tunnels beneath his mountain city of Veridia had been gruelling, dirty, and most of all, tiring. Amidst the desolate landscape, he could see remnants of ancient structures, half-buried, forgotten by time. Crumbling stone walls and weathered statues stood as silent witnesses to the destructive nature of nature itself. As his ascent continued, he could see the distant summit looming faintly, shrouded in a thick plume of smoke.

His face felt grimy, a feeling that only weeks after weeks on the trail could do to a man. His once pale skin was now caked in dust and dirt, but his eyes, like twin orbs of burning emeralds, still glowed with an inner fire of the brightest of green. A once well-groomed beard now overgrown, covered his face. His black hair, which fell to his shoulders in a controlled tangle, blew behind him as each gust of wind that went past. Thankfully his simple silver chain still rested, secure around his neck. It was the last thing he had to remember his father by, with his kingdom now gone. The chain had been in his family since the days of the conquering, and he wasn't going to leave that for the rebels.

His steps were heavy, as he followed the mysterious figure. They had called him a tyrant and a despot. Those peasants. They did not have the knowledge, intelligence or wherewithal to understand he was only protecting them. Those damnable barbarians of the northern highlands and of the great southern forest, the rats of the far southern sands and the freaks in the mountains to the east, all of them out for the blood of his good people. This stranger had told him he could help him regain his throne, but how? He couldn't just walk into the throne room and seize it, he had no army, few supporters, no power. Something here, within the ruins ahead, would give him the edge he would need for his reconquest.

"You've been taught the story of the ruins ahead of us?" The figure asked from ahead.

"Everyone has. The ruins of Emberfell, the kingdom that ruled all, now just a collection of cinders."

Printed in Dunstable, United Kingdom